100 Not Out

100 Not Out

Gordon Lawrie

Comely Bank Publishing

First published 2016
by Comely Bank Publishing

This paperback edition published 2017

ISBN 978-0-9930262-4-9

Original cover design by Learmonth Design
Text printed in Garamond

A CIP catalogue record for this book is available from the British Library.

Contents

FOREWORD

Some years ago, I started up a discussion thread in a writers' group, asking people to contribute flash fiction.

As it was a Friday (and I love alliteration), I called the thread Friday Flash Fiction – and lo, a movement was born. The thread became a website, a blog and eventually a group of its own.

Gordon Lawrie has always been a champion and a stalwart of the Friday Flash Fiction movement. He set up the website and he contributes a short story every week, without fail. This book is a collection of some of his finest flash fiction and I'm sure everyone will find a story that chimes with their own experiences.

There are stories that will make you shake your head in recognition, satire that will make you wince and some odd flights of fancy involving dragons, cats, life on Pluto and of course golf. Most of all, though, you will probably laugh. Gordon has a keen sense of humour and that definitely shows in his writing. I defy you to read the whole book and not to laugh out loud at least once.

Once you've read the book, I'd urge you to try out Gordon's sense of humour in longer form – *Four Geezers and a Valkyrie* is a cracking good read.

Finally, do you have some flash fiction in you? If so, Gordon and I entreat you become part of the Friday Flash Fiction movement. You'll find the website at www.fridayflashfiction. com if you'd like to join in.

Emma Baird, May 2016

INTRODUCTION

Followers of social media will be aware of LinkedIn, best described as Facebook for business folk. There they parade their wares, their skills, generally show off and fall out with each other in just the same way as people do on Facebook, Twitter, Instagram or whatever the latest hip medium is. Occasionally you might be offered a job totally unsuited to your CV, but it's not a place you expect to make good friends.

As a struggling (for which read 'failed') author and would-be publisher back in August 2013, I was trawling through LinkedIn trying to pick up some tips in this bear pit when I stumbled across a 'Discussion' started by Emma Baird, who it later transpired lived only 40 miles or so away. She'd thrown out a challenge to anyone and everyone to write a story of no more than 100 words, not including the title, and post it the following Friday.

Someone did. Then another, then another, then another until eventually thousands upon thousands of stories had been submitted. One of those who submitted was me, and because Emma makes a point of welcoming all newcomers individually I was encouraged to write more, not only every Friday but on other days, too. I discovered that people liked to listen to these super-short stories, and whenever I did an author event to promote my book and other writing I found my own personal 100-word stories kept the audience entertained, or at least from falling asleep.

By now, I'd formed a self-publishing cooperative which published not only my own first novel but several other books besides, including Emma Baird's own first novel, and along the way I found that I'd not only acquired a very good friend, she'd become my closest literary confidante and adviser. The only problem turned out to be that writing flash fiction was in itself a real distraction from *serious writing*, and I've ended up with six or seven half-written 'difficult second novels' as Emma likes to refer to them.

Meanwhile, the 'used' 100-word yarns disappeared into an archive where they remained forgotten, and it was only when I recently opened up a folder on my laptop that I discovered that I myself had written hundreds of these things without being aware of it.

So here's a small selection, exactly 100, for your amusement. I've divided them into categories although quite a few could pop up in more than one, so it's a bit arbitrary. Each story is exactly 100 words long on Word's wordcount, which counts hyphenated words as one. You might occasionally feel that's cheating. For me, that's a frankly-my-dear-I-don't-give-damn situation. (That last sentence therefore has six words.) Either way, they're for reading in a little book or on your ereader on the bus or last thing before you go to bed at night, and you can safely read something like *War And Peace* simultaneously as your light relief. I hope you enjoy reading them as much as I enjoyed writing them.

Gordon Lawrie, May 2016

THE
STORIES

Crime And Justice

RAVENNA TO BOLOGNA, OCTOBER 2013

This was actually the very first story I ever wrote for Friday Flash Fiction.

I recently found myself on a return train from Ravenna to Bologna in northern Italy. Confused, I'd messed up validating the ticket on the outward journey, but the friendly train conductor wrote a note on the ticket for the conductor on the journey home. That way I wouldn't incur a huge fine.

But coming back, the train conductor didn't speak any English, and my Italian wasn't good enough either. Exasperated, I kept saying 'Non copisco'; exasperated, he kept shouting louder and louder.

So I did the only thing possible. I took a gun from my jacket and shot him dead.

ALL IN THE NAME OF?

It was all over in minutes.

The two men had been arrested, tried, found guilty and condemned, all in accordance with law. A crowd had gathered near the gallows. No children, though.

Someone pronounced a few official words. The condemned pair, their hands tied behind their backs, were led up some steps to a narrow wooden table, and a noose placed around each man's neck.

Then the table was kicked away. They didn't quite die immediately, it took a minute or so; afterwards, two small pools of urine could be seen below.

Their crime? They loved each other, of course.

THE HANGING JUDGE

For St Andrew's Day.

In the dock, the prisoner stood, ready for the inevitable. The judge studied him sternly.

'Prisoner,' she said, 'you have been found guilty of failing to write a story for Friday Flash Fiction today. Have you anything to say?'

'No, ma'am,' he bleated.

The judge excitedly fumbled for her black cap.

'In that case, I hereby sentence you to be hanged by the feet in the public square until you've thought something up.'

Someone in the gallery cried 'No!' The prisoner bowed his head, knowing that as a kilt-wearing Scot, his darkest secret could no longer be kept hidden.

THE BODY IN THE LIBRARY

Holmes studied the victim's body in the library. Head beaten with a blunt instrument. Blood, yes, but also water on the carpet. No murder weapon.

'I'm baffled,' Watson said. 'It's cold in here.'

Suddenly, Holmes leapt to his feet. 'It's elementary, Watson!'

'Elementary?'

'The butler did it,' said Holmes. 'Ring for him!'

Moments later the butler, Jeeves, appeared. 'You rang, sir?'

'You beat the victim to death with a block of ice, which melted. As butler, Jeeves, you're the only one with access to ice.'

Jeeves bowed. 'As you wish, sir.' Then he added, 'Shall I bring the handcuffs, sir?'

SUMMARY JUSTICE

'No!' Chelsea yelled. 'Put me down! Let me go! Stop!'

She felt herself being hoisted into the air, and with no great care either.

'It isn't fair, it's not my fault! Why me?' she moaned. 'I'm not even two years old yet – '

She was cut off in mid-sentence.

It made no difference, because no-one could understand what Chelsea the Range Rover was saying as she was lowered into the crusher, her owner having repeatedly been caught speeding on the school run. Some observers even applauded.

It's not fair on the car. It's the owner who belongs in the crusher.

ABRAHAM ZAPRUDER

For the 50th anniversary of President Kennedy's assassination. Abraham Zapruder captured the famous live footage of the event.

I got it, I got it!

I got the whole thing in my movie camera. It's all in there.

I was watching the President, the shots came from behind my back.

I'm gonna be rich, I'm gonna be famous.

Everyone will want a piece of me.

What's gonna happen?

The police will want to speak to me. The papers, the TV. Everyone.

Maybe I don't wanna be rich and famous.

They say the camera never lies. I wish it did this time.

I think I'll give all my cameras away.

I don't like cameras any more.

THE CUT THROAT GANG

It took the Cut Throat Gang just three minutes to steal seven hundred thousand pounds from the West End branch of the Bank of Scotland. Forty seconds to smash through the front door, twenty seconds to disable all the alarms, one minute thirty seconds to crack the safe, thirty seconds to scoop all the money into bags before they made their escape.

It took a lot less than three minutes to catch them. Thanks to a tip-off, the police were waiting for them at the door as they came out.

THE HACKER

Martha stared at her computer. The enormity of her achievement had finally dawned on her.

Aged just seventeen, she'd hacked into one of the world's biggest banks. She'd simply become the Royal Bank of Scotland. All that remained was to transfer money from the RBS account into an unmarked Swiss account that only she knew about.

Typing in the last steps, the screen greeted her: 'Welcome, RBS. What service would you like?' She asked it to transfer ten thousand pounds to Switzerland.

There was a delay, then the screen said simply, 'Sorry RBS, you have insufficient funds for this transaction.'

DISSIDENT

Refused permission by the authorities to write in his native language, the dissident decided to mark his opposition in two ways. Firstly, he published his latest story in picture-form: a piece of flash fiction expressed as a strip cartoon, the only words being those found in billboard signs, newspaper headlines and so on. Secondly, he posted a 'real' hundred-word story on the a website he himself had created. Those who wanted to read it would know where to find it.

The effect was electric: the story went viral, until one day there was a knock on his apartment front door.

ON THE NAUGHTY STEP

They both sat on the naughty step. She'd been argumentative – something about snakes – he'd been name-calling.

''S a' yer fault ah'm here,' she moaned. ''S no' fair.'

'Yous is aye cliping,' he grumped. 'If it wisnae fur yous, we'd neither o' us be here. Twenty minutes! Naw, s'no fair right enough.'

Meanwhile, Maw was in the kitchen making dinner. 'Quiet, yous twa!' she yelled. 'D'ye's want some mair?'

The bairns replied in chorus that 'it wisnae fair, it wis the other yin's fault.' That did it, twenty minutes more. They protested, but Maw was unmoved. The cat wasn't impressed, either.

THE SUPREME COURT RULES

The garden game quickly descended into a squabble about the rules. Minutes later, Mom was there to sort it out.

'He cheated!' the girl said.

'That true?' Mom asked.

''Plead the 5th,' the boy said.

'He's a dirty low-down cheat!' the girl said.

Mom said, 'Don't speak like – '

'I'll say what I like: 1st Amendment.' Bear in mind these two kids are six and four.

'Well,' said Mom, 'Mrs Walker's phoned to complain – '

'That old witch!' the kids said in unison.

That did it. They were over her knee in no time: a cruel but not unusual punishment.

MORNING BREAK WITH THE BOYS

Following a ridiculous ruling by England's Justice Minister that prisoners should not be allowed to receive books in prison, I donated some new copies of my own for the local prison library. They invited me to take a tour.

It's ten o'clock.

I'm looking down a long corridor. Because it's tea-break time, hundreds of people like me are walking from one part of the building to another. Gym to library. Farm area to education area. Anywhere to pass just another little part of the morning.

Everyone's in uniform, although not the same uniform. Some in red, some in blue, some in green; a cynical group wear jackets and carry radios.

You wouldn't like it here. I don't, which I suppose is the point.

Actually, come to think of it, could you remind me again exactly what the point IS?

BREAK-IN AT THE DEAD OF NIGHT

0400 hours. Finally, the culmination of months of planning.

With one last hammer blow from Jake, the wall gave way and the Cut-Throat Gang found themselves on the ground floor of Pyramid, the high-end jewellers in Edinburgh's West End. In front of them sat the diamond ring mounted in platinum, worth countless thousands, that they had all set their heart on.

Jake stepped forward to look closer; the price-tag said 'Special Price Today - £1.00 only.' He smiled.

A voice spoke behind him. 'Jake, isn't this taking it a bit far to be first in the queue for Black Friday?'

WHITE LILIES

This is on exactly the same subject as the Billie Holiday song 'Strange Fruit'.

Tick, tock, tick, tock. I look up as the pendulum swings.

Back and forward, back and forward.

I'm out at night with my sister, a few years older than me. From a safe distance, we're watching a familiar scene from the thirties: a solitary tree in a field, a bunch of white lilies stand below, silently gazing up as the tree keeps its own slow, rhythmic beat. The branch creaks in perfect time.

Back and forward.

My sister touches my arm. 'Watch, Ellen,' she whispers in my ear. 'Watch the lilies.'

'Aren't lilies supposed to be beautiful?' I ask her.

GUYS AND DOLLS

Barbie stood on the corner, chewing gum authoritatively. Most of the gang were dressed in short skirts and low-slung tops, but Barbie's demeanour marked her out clearly as leader.

'Hey dolls, time to hit the clubs,' she said.

Nodding towards a figure standing a little away, Steffi and Cindy screwed up their faces. 'All of us?'

'Why not?' A command, not a question. 'He can't help being male.'

'The inferior 49%,' Steffi muttered.

They set off, Action Man a few paces behind. Then he drew out his machine gun and wasted them all.

'The violent 49%. You dolls never learn.'

History

4th AUGUST, 1914
VECTORS
CHEZ CAESAR
TRAITORS
A.D. 1582
BURMA, 1944
ORVILLE AND WILBUR FLIGHT
RUSSIAN LEFT BOOT DAY

4th AUGUST, 1914

All the boys in the village were excited by the news. 'It'll be an adventure,' they said. 'We'll all join up together.'

'Don't go,' said Alice, but she was torn. She worried a little, but she was so proud of them, and she didn't need to be told that two of the most handsome ones, Danny and Carlos, had a shine for her. They were already competing for her attention, trying to show who was the bravest.

'Don't be afraid for us,' the boys said. 'Anyway, we'll be back in no time.'

That wasn't how it worked out, of course.

VECTORS

If you can recall your school mathematics lessons, 'vectors' are distances to which direction has been applied. Their practical use really only dates from the mid-eighteenth century, but they're known as 'Euclidean' vectors because it was the ancient Greek mathematician Euclid who first spotted their importance.

A keen runner, he ran in the 10,000 metres finals at the 272BC Olympics. Trailing in a distant ninth, Euclid suddenly realised that after a great deal of effort running 25 laps, he was simply back where he'd started.

Euclid thus proved it was more efficient to be a couch potato than a runner.

CHEZ CAESAR

The other night four of us hit The Colosseum, the classiest joint in town. The waiter showed us to our table.

'What'ya got?' I asked. 'Any of that stuff you had on the menu last time?'

'Christian?' the waiter replied. 'Sure, sir, fresh in from Spain.'

'Spain?' Leo said. 'Different – you certain it's good?'

'The best, sir. 'Animal even has a name – 'Maximus'. Tonight, we're serving it garlic-infused with a side salad.'

'Yeah? OK, waiter – Maximus for four! Make it snappy.'

The Colosseum didn't let us down. Twenty minutes later, we four shared a great meal.

Scrunch, scrunch, scrunch.

Yum.

TRAITORS

During and after World War Two, Britain's Secret Intelligence Service MI6 was infiltrated by Soviet double agents. Four were eventually identified: Burgess (codename 'Hicks'), Maclean ('Homer'), Philby ('Stanley') and Blunt ('Johnson'), but rumours continued regarding the final member of the infamous 'Cambridge Five'. The recent movie 'The Imitation Game' suggested John Cairncross, without foundation.

We can now exclusively reveal the fifth spy. Sir Nicholas de Lapland was ideal: a bearded, unremarkable older man moving quietly in society. The perfect spy is seen but ignored.

Perhaps the colour of codename 'Santa's' unusual cape should have indicated his likely political leanings, however.

A.D. 1582

A.D. 1582: Pope Gregory put down his pen. At last, after years of trying, he had produced his first ever flash fiction story – and finished it on a Friday, as well. It was a story about his favourite subject: time.

Logging into LinkedIn, he copied and pasted his contribution into the Friday Flash Fiction discussion, only to be greeted with howls of complaint from others that he'd got the day wrong. It wasn't Friday, but actually Monday. Not according to the chart on HIS wall, though.

'Ah,' he said to himself. 'Looks like I need to change the calendar, then.'

BURMA, 1944

Not technically fiction, I suppose. If my dad hadn't been one of the six, you wouldn't be reading this now.

The doctors and nurses have all been led outside the tent by the Japanese; we, the wounded, are left to wonder inside.

Suddenly there's a long burst of machine-gun fire, followed by a silence, then some Japanese shouting.

Then another brief silence.

Suddenly the machine gun is strafing our tent we dive below most of us too late but not me thank God.

Silence.

A Japanese soldier enters the tent, searching for the living. Bullet to the head each time. I play dead.

Six of us escape under cover of darkness later.

I suppose our side does bad stuff too.

ORVILLE AND WILBUR FLIGHT

Orville and Wilbur Flight stood at the fifth-floor window, ready to try their man-powered flight machine. Like the ill-fated Icarus Project, the pilot was required to pedal a bike which by complex gearing powered fast-flapping wings on the pilot's back.

Orville produced a coin. 'Toss to see who goes first. Heads you win.' He tossed: heads.

'Great!' said an excited Wilbur, and without further ado donned the contraption and launched into thin air pedalling furiously. Immediately, he plunged fifty feet to his death.

'At last,' said Orville, pocketing the double-headed coin. 'Now I'm the sole heir to the family fortune.'

RUSSIAN LEFT BOOT DAY

You're probably aware that today is 'Russian Left Boot Day', a long-running celebration of a wartime episode when the Soviet central planning system went disastrously wrong.

During WW2, boots for Soviet soldiers were in such short supply that Stalin ordered one million pairs to be made immediately. Unfortunately, he wasn't specific enough, and instead of one million pairs, two million left boots were made.

Everyone was too scared while he was alive, but since Stalin's death, self-deprecating Russians have celebrated this day every year by wearing left shoes on both feet all day.

Watch out for iPhone 'selfies' being posted...

Art And Literature

IN AN OFFICE SOMEWHERE
AN IMAGINARY AUDITION
HARD TIMES
PRIDE AND PREJUDICE, FINGER-
LICKIN' STYLE
PRIDE AND PREJUDICE N' A SINGLE
DEEP-FRIED MARS BAR
THE VISITING SPEAKER
A QUOTE FROM THE PAINTER
THE CRITIC
OZ REVISITED
METAMORPHOSIS
THE WILLIAMS FAMILY AND THE
TWIN-NECKED FOURTEEN-STRING
BANJO
INSIDE THE LOUVRE
(PRIDE AND PREJUDICE) ON THE No36
BUS
DEL'S INSPIRED MOMENT

IN AN OFFICE SOMEWHERE

The publisher sighed. He'd not been looking forward to this meeting with the author.

'This book of yours, 'How To Pass Mathematics Examinations'. There's a problem. Quite a few, I'm afraid.'

The author bristled. 'Such as?'

'Well, it says here two plus two equals five. That'll have to go.'

'Why?'

'Because it's not right. And triangles don't have four sides. And you can't fill π with chicken.'

'I'm the mathematician. I know these things. I have a degree.'

'From where?'

'Pluto. University College. A 2:1. Tell me, where's YOUR mathematics degree from?'

The publisher sighed. 'I don't have one.'

'SEEEE!!!!!'

AN IMAGINARY AUDITION

'Mr Bell? I'm Frederic Chopin. I've come for the... audition.'

'Come in, sit down please.'

'So what's the gig, Mr Bell?'

'Look, Freddie, this telephone I've invented – thing is, now we need jingles, tunes that play when you're hanging on the line for ages. Must be really short.'

'Why?'

'So they play repeatedly and get annoying. You do short stuff?'

'The Minute Waltz.'

'Too long. Do you have a Half-A-Minute Waltz?'

'A Demi-Minute Waltz? Sorry, no.'

'Can't you play your Minute Waltz twice as fast?'

'Suppose so.'

'Perfect – you've got the gig. It'll sell like hot-cakes in the call centres.'

HARD TIMES

Back in 1959, found myself bummin' around Minnesota way, playing guitar and singing songs to earn my next meal. Truth was, I could barely read or write then.

I remember running into this nasally-voiced little guy with curly hair who sang folk songs. We swapped a few things; I gave him one of mine about stuff blowin' in the wind, he gave me one called 'We Shall Overcome'. Turned out that wasn't even his. I think he used mine, though.

Later, someone else took a kinda pop-song of mine called 'She Loves You'. Never found out what happened to that.

PRIDE AND PREJUDICE, FINGER-LICKIN' STYLE

I remember the day Bingley and the Darcy guy hit town like it were yesterday. Bingley was looking for chicks; the Darcy guy was harder to read. Soon they'd landed with the Bennet girls, although neither Ol' Man Bennet nor his wife had any swing with their daughters.

Anyway, Bingley and the eldest girl Jane hung out, but the next one, called Lizzie, was tougher. Hot with a Winchester. But Darcy pulled her; Lizzie picked up a bad apple in that guy Wickham and Darcy rode to the rescue.

These days Darcy and Lizzie live on that big ranch Pemberley.

PRIDE AND PREJUDICE N' A SINGLE DEEP-FRIED MARS BAR, A' WI' SALT'nVINEGAR PLEASE

Bingley and Darcy swanned in lookin' fur lumber. Bingley got aff wi' Jane Bennett; Lizzie telt Darcy tae awa'n bile his heid. Yon Bennet lassies, mind, were ootae control. But Darcy 'n Lizzie? Ach, wan wis as bad as the ither. Meanwhile Collins, who'd bag off wi' onythin in skirts, ended up wi Charlotte.

Onewise, they a' skirled aboot dancin' awhile, there wis sum stuff wi' Lydia and a nyaff ca'd Wickham so Darcy paid them tae get married. Lizzie was fair cowpit, married Darcy and ended in yon big hoose!

In Scotland there'd have been a pagger fur sure.

THE VISITING SPEAKER

The storytellers' group sat in a circle, listening politely to the visiting speaker. He'd spoken for well over twenty minutes. Most of them were beginning to feel their eyes glaze over as he'd outlined his past history, then gone on to read some of his work. Some of the group were beginning to shuffle in their seats to relieve the discomfort in their behinds.

But a small number who were paying the greatest attention had begun to notice subtle changes in the appearance and behaviour of their guest.

Then they realised he had stopped speaking and become a giant penguin.

A QUOTE FROM THE DECORATORS

- 'Hi, Pops! Nice to hear from you!'

- 'You wanna go ahead with the job? Sure? Whaddayawant on the ceiling? Plain white?'

- 'Pictures? Jeez, Pops, ceiling paper on a curved ceiling's tough. It'll cost.'

- 'You what, Pops?'

- 'You want some pics of Bible scenes painted by HAND up there? Sixty feet up? I'll need scaffolding, Pops.'

- 'Really? Just send you the bill? OK, but gold halo paint prices are pretty high just now. What pics d'ya want?'

- 'Whatever I like?'

- 'No, I don't do smiling women. That's the other guy, Pops.'

- 'Sorry, Pops, I can't 'throw in a helicopter' for free.'

THE CRITIC

He waited for the appropriate response.

Sure enough she said, as programmed, 'You are quite right, Master. My work has no meaning. It is worthless. I am worthless.'

He continued to gaze out of the window. 'And it does not meet the requirements you were set,' he added.

She intoned, 'You are quite right, Master. I did not meet the requirements as set. My work is worthless. I am worthless.'

He decided he was done. 'You are dismissed.' She left immediately.

He smiled in satisfaction. At least he could criticise intelligently even if he himself could produce nothing of value.

OZ REVISITED

By now, Dorothy had collected quite an army: a lion, a dragon, a grizzly bear, a straw man and a tin man on her journey to see the Wizard of Oz seeking help in confronting the resurgent Wicked Witch Of The South-West. This might previously have caused problems for arm-linked sixsomes, but the intervening years had seen The Yellow Brick Road expanded into a ten-lane inter-state highway. They were there in no time.

'What d'ya want now?' the irritated Wizard drawled. Dorothy explained, patiently.

'Her?' the Wizard replied. 'Just threaten her with a parking ticket. She'll be a quivering wreck.'

METAMORPHOSIS

With apologies to Franz Kafka...

Gregor woke from troubled dreams to discover that he was eight months pregnant. Transformed in his bed, he lay on his back, and if he lifted his head a little he could see his large belly, slightly domed. The bedding was hardly able to cover it and seemed ready to slide off any moment. He had developed breasts, and such was his size that he could barely move.

'What's happened to me? It must be a dream,' he thought, and tried to turn over and sleep. But it wasn't a dream.

He shook his head. 'I must stop eating kebabs.'

THE WILLIAMS FAMILY
AND THE TWIN-NECKED
FOURTEEN-STRING BANJO

Kentucky's Williams family had a unique claim to fame: only they could play the extraordinary twin-necked fourteen-string banjo. Essentially, it was two five-stringers, with two extra drone strings in cavities in each neck's back. One neck was tuned in fourths F-B-E-A-D-G-C, the other in fifths, G-D-A-E-B-F-C.

Famous tunes included 'Kentucky 14-String Hoe-Down' and 'Kentucky Williams Blues', playable only by family members with unusually long fingers. Some experts think they had Marfans Syndrome, but it might have been inbreeding: they always married cousins.

In the 1960s the Williams started to marry out; nowadays the extraordinary music is limited to old recordings.

INSIDE THE LOUVRE

Why do people stare? – It's so rude. They stare at me, so I stare back at them. Then more people wander up, they stare at me, too, so I stare back at them as well.

They talk about me; they want to know what I'm thinking, but that's my business, not theirs. They don't even speak in Italian – not so much as a 'Ciao, Lisa'.

You wonder why I'm smiling? I'll tell you. Every day, thousands of people who know nothing about art pay around fifteen euros to come and stare at me.

That's a smile of contempt, trust me.

ON THE No.36 BUS

On the lower deck of the bus, Roseanne sat reading *Pride And Prejudice*.

Across the isle, three women discussed fridge contents – fruit, chicken needing to be used, some broccoli.

Behind Roseanne, two men discussed fingernail-clipping and shaving techniques. However, their switch of topics to deodorants was just too much for her.

'Shut the **** up! I'm trying to read!'

As instructed, everyone was immediately silent; fourteen faces turned towards Roseanne unblinkingly. Then the whispering started.

'Who does she think she is?'

'I've got a Kindle.'

'I've read *50 Shades*.'

'What's reading?'

Roseanne sighed, shut her book, then closed her eyes.

DEL'S INSPIRED MOMENT

Early on, a visitor to LinkedIn's Friday Flash Fiction thread posted a comment to say that our grammar, spelling and so on were poor, and offering his services (for a fee) to edit the stories. He was too soft a target, really.

Del scratched his head. He'd never heard of 'flash fiction' before, was keen to join in, but what exactly *was* it? A type of story about night-time photography? A type of story for perverts? A type of story about lighthouses? None of these offered much scope for inspiration.

All he needed was a hundred words, no more.

Suddenly, it came to him: the instructions contained a typo which would have been spotted if they'd been properly proofread. It should read 'flash *friction*'.

Shaking his head, he drew a match from a box in his pocket and struck it. Job done.

Love and Romance

LOVE STORY No. 1

Their meal was expensive, but worth it; afterwards, they walked down to the harbour, then out along the pier. Gazing upwards, she realised how much city street lights generally prevented her from seeing the night sky.

Reading her mind perfectly, he said, 'Lovely night. The steak was done to perfection.'

'That's Orion,' she said.

'That German pinot noir was amazing,' he agreed. 'I was slightly doubtful when I saw the price, but it was great, wasn't it?'

'Is that a planet?' she wondered, nuzzling into him, putting her arm around his waist. Then: 'I love you.'

'Me too,' he said.

LOVE, SCOTTISH-STYLE

The skin-headed fascist Scottish thug yelled at his upstairs Polish neighbour.

'Away back tae yer ain country, ya bam!'

'Leave him alane,' the thug's pregnant girlfriend cried, 'he means nae harm!'

'Away you and shut up,' the thug shouted. He drew her closer, then grabbed her by the neck, kicked her, forced her down, then kicked her again repeatedly in the stomach as she lay curled up on the floor. Fortunately at that moment the police appeared to save her.

As the police took his statement, the thug said, 'I went too far, I only wanted to propose to her.'

LOVE STORY No. 3

Arlene gazes at the skies. 'Its going to be a beautiful day,' she says.

Her boyfriend Rab, a dour Scot, grunts, 'Aye, right.'

Arlene's confused. 'Isn't that an oxymoron, Robert? You said 'yes' twice.' She's not Scottish and understands neither it's people nor it's language.

'No, its just an oxy, its not a moron. 'Aye right' means no.'

Suddenly the heavens open. Arlene seems sure to get soaked but suddenly Rab produces an umbrella big enough for them both.

'I'll never understand you, but I love you,' she says, gazing at him.

'You'll never understand the weather either, will you?'

A FINE ROMANCE

The evening was going well.

They'd met through www.findmyperfectmate. com; now they sat in a city-centre cafe. Mark called Shelley 'brainy', but he was pretty intelligent himself.

They shared many interests – books, music, and unusual foods – kidney, liver and – remarkably – sweetbreads. The evening flew by.

She considered inviting Mark to her flat, but decided that it was too soon. Instead – to his disappointment – she settled for a shop-doorway lingering kiss.

Suddenly, he pulled away. 'Have you ever experienced a Norwegian kiss?'

'No. Go on.' She closed her eyes expectantly.

Her body was discovered next day, minus all of its internal organs.

ROMANTIC FIREWORKS ON 5th NOVEMBER

'Hi there.'

'Hi. Weren't you here last year?'

'Must have been someone that looked just like me. My name's Roman.'

'Mine's Catherine. Roman? That Polish?'

'Chinese, actually. Not long arrived in the country.'

'Me too. Look, could you give me a little breathing space? I'm feeling rather pinned to the wall here.'

'Oh sorry. Thoughtless of me.'

'Not your fault. This stranger came by, we started talking, then suddenly he was off like a rocket.'

'How rude.'

'Unlike you – you seem to have some sparkle. Have you got a light by any chance?'

'Sorry, I'm trying to give up smoking.'

LOVE IN THE TWENTY-FIRST CENTURY

As daylight filtered through half-open curtains, Alison and Martin made love once more. Enjoying the afterglow fifteen minutes later, Alison reflected that practice was making her man perfect. Having him round to stay over three times weekly was working.

Suddenly, her mother shrieked from downstairs. 'Alison! Time to get up.'

Quickly, she ushered a rapidly-dressing Martin out via the bedroom window and the garage roof. Alison, meanwhile, showered, dressed and casually wandered downstairs.

Without looking up from his newspaper, her father said, 'Will we meet Martin some time?'

'Not yet,' Alison said. 'I'm not ready for that level of commitment.'

TENDER IS THE NIGHT

Christine studied the man lying with his back to her, asleep.

She smiled. She knew she should probably get up and go to the bathroom, but she wanted to retain the moment for as long as possible. The bed linen could wait until morning; it had been worth it.

John had taken her – probably both of them, to be honest – to a place she hadn't been for years, had thought perhaps she wouldn't ever visit again. He knew: he always insisted that he could tell from the glow around her neck.

Thank goodness life continued to be full of surprises.

DINNER ON ST VALENTINE'S DAY

When he returned from being out, she had his dinner ready to eat on the table, and she knew he was happy. The table was laid out beautifully, adorned with red roses that she'd chosen lovingly for him, and she'd cooked chicken, his favourite, poached gently for twenty minutes just as he liked it.

It being Valentine's Day, she'd dressed for the occasion; she wore his favourite dress, a red velour figure-hugging piece that she'd picked up in a boutique the previous year. As he studied her, she smiled: how she loved him.

Alice would do anything for her cat.

THE PRICE OF LOVE

They'd met on the internet. Their first date really couldn't have gone any better; glorious food in a wonderful restaurant. He paid, and they made to leave.

'Your place or mine?' he asked at the door.

'Not tonight, not yet,' she breathed softly. 'Next time, I promise. Let's part here tonight.'

He sighed, then smiled. 'Spoilsport,' and hailed a cab for her.

'Kiss me,' she said. 'Kiss me like we're making love. Now.' The taxi driver waited.

Later, alone in the taxi, she reflected on her evening: a wallet, credit cards, a Rolex watch and four pounds twenty-six in change.

AN AGE-OLD STORY

Through the park they walked. They sat on a bench, ambled around the pond, then found their favourite quiet spot. Soon, they were as one, legs entwined.

'I love you,' he said. 'Will you marry me?'

She looked doubtful. 'Is it allowed?'

'Don't you want to share your life with me?'

She stammered, 'Yes, but – '

He looked away. 'Is it because I'm a frog?' he snapped. 'Am I not good enough?'

'Of course not. I'm a frog too. Don't be silly.' It was her turn to be upset.

They had this conversation every day.

Post coitum, omne triste est.

HER FINAL MEAL

'Can I get you anything?' I asked her. She'd been flitting in and out of sleep, and looked tired. She struggled a smile saying, 'I could perhaps eat something.'

I knew what was required. First I dry-fried a cinnamon stick, ground cloves and cardamom seeds, added a little oil then gently sautéed some sliced onion. Next, I browned some diced chicken then added coriander, cummin, fenugreek, turmeric, ginger, garlic, chilli, salt and some chicken stock. Twenty minutes later, I served it with basmati rice.

'Ah,' she said, 'to die for.'

It was like this every week. Next Friday, beef curry.

HAPPY ANNIVERSARY, DARLING

For their anniversary, they'd bought each other printed tee-shirts. She'd bought him a black shirt with a Harley-Davidson motorbike on the front; he'd bought her a specially-made white thing bearing his own face, gazing upwards Ché Guevara-style.

'Oh, how lovely,' they said in unison, although she'd opened her present first.

'I thought you might wear me out,' he grinned. 'Get the joke?'

She reflected on the passing of another year. Five years of marriage, five anniversary presents: a mop, a toilet-seat, a year's car insurance, and last year's humdinger, a budgerigar. All things considered, she'd got off lightly this time.

DAVID AND MARCIA, A LOVE STORY

In memory of our near-neighbours.

David and Marcia's retirement was never active. On summer evenings they sat outside on folding chairs, greeting neighbours and passing strangers alike. They measured time not in hours and minutes, but in 'gin-and-tonic inches', glasses refilling miraculously without either of them ever moving.

Marcia smoked like a chimney and used her low gravelly voice to boss David about and make grand pronouncements about the declining state of the country. Neighbours simply smiled benignly.

But David loved her, and when Marcia's heart suddenly gave out, he faded away within months. They're together now, I'm sure; their ashes are, at any rate.

BREAKFAST ON ST VALENTINE'S DAY

On St Valentine's Day they had breakfast in bed: scrambled eggs topped with smoked salmon, and Buck's Fizz. To save washing, they fed each other naked. It was just an excuse.

Drizzling Buck's Fizz over her, he gazed into her eyes. 'Have I ever told you I love you?' he asked.

'Occasionally,' she said. 'Do you know how much I love you?'

'I've got the idea,' he said.

He kissed her feet; she kissed his in return.

'I could eat you alive,' he said.

'Mmm. Me too.'

And so they did. The last couple of mouthfuls were a little tricky.

LOVE DOWN THE DRAIN

Eric the drain stood erect just a couple of feet from his partner Kerry.

'We drains belong together in the world,' he said. 'We're already living together - can't we just tie the knot?'

Kerry stood impassively. 'I think we work better this way, doing our own thing,' she said.

Just then, a bath began to empty. As the water coursed through her, Kerry's beautiful voice echoed in the night sky.

'You and I could make such sweet music together, Kerry,' Eric said, just as someone flushed a toilet in the same bathroom.

Kerry smiled. 'Eric, you're so full of – '

ILL-STARRED BY MOONLIGHT

They'd met in a club, a holiday romance; one thing had led to another.

They lay on the beach in the warm night.

'I love you, Claire,' Asif said. 'Will you marry me?'

She knew he wasn't being serious. 'I love you, too. But my parents will only let me marry a prince.' That wasn't the real problem, of course. 'Let's count the stars together instead.'

Asif took the sky on the left. They counted 714.

'I've got an idea,' he said. 'Let's elope.'

'Where to?'

'I have friends on Pluto.'

'That's it, then,' said Claire. They kissed on it.

Science, Technology and Science Fiction

IN THE NEAR FUTURE
PERSONAL SERVICES
IN-FLIGHT ENTERTAINMENT
UNECLIPSE
WRONG TURNING TO THE MOON
DOES FLASH GORDON LIVE HERE?
DOES EVERYONE GET THESE?
IT'S WRITTEN IN THE STARS

IN THE NEAR FUTURE

Planning for a world population of eight billion is not straightforward.

First, it's necessary to make mobile phones, iPads, Skype and built-in cameras desired by everyone. GPS tracking is easy. Then comes the tricky bit: develop fingerprint and face recogniton, accurate enough to link to that GPS tracking. The population collaborates willingly, telling everyone on Facebook, Instagram and Twitter what they're doing. The entire world's activities are recorded.

One last problem: there's mountains of data about who's meeting whom, who's working where, who's sleeping with whom. It's too much. How to proceed?

Easy. Pick on the people you don't like.

PERSONAL SERVICES

Hi there.

You know what I need from you, don't you? That's it – just slide it in there, where I need it, just there... perfect.

You know what to do next as well. Only you know how to press my buttons... so perfectly.

Now tell me what you need... touch me there... perfect.

While I serve your needs, do you need a receipt for my services? No? That's fine. There you go now, take what you need from me.

Are you satisfied? Do you need any more?

(As spoken by 'Samantha' one of the new generation of talking cash dispensers.)

IN-FLIGHT ENTERTAINMENT

Far into Andromeda, Agnes looked out of the window.

'I wonder what it was really like flying those cramped old space rockets,' she said. 'How did they stand it? No shower, no pool first thing in the morning. Ugh!'

Charlotte nodded. 'It took so LONG. Thank God we live in the age of megalightspeed travel. When are we due to land?'

'A couple of hours more, Charlie,' Agnes said. 'Time you were going. How long have you got, by the way?'

'The room's booked for forty minutes.'

Charlotte set off to fetch that Australian from the top deck. He'd do.

UNECLIPSE

The child grumbled. 'What's so special about a total uneclipse?'

His mother sighed. 'I'll explain again. We live on Pluto, right on the edge of the solar system. Other stuff – planets, moons, asteroids, Saturn's rings – keep blocking out the sun, which we actually orbit. We only see the sun in rare uneclipses.'

Suddenly, the sky was lit by the brightest thing either of them had ever seen; the distant sun transformed even Pluto in a wondrous light-show. Just fourteen dazzling minutes later it was over.

'So? That's it?' the child said. 'Can I PLEASE go back to my Playstation now?'

WRONG TURNING TO THE MOON

It was only as she looked out of the cockpit window that Rawgug realised her terrible error.

'@@@$$%%%!!£%(*&**'   she   cried. '?^&&^&&^&'

Her co-pilot Malwog did as directed, adding, '°¬^ø•¶!'

Realising they would now be stranded on the Moon instead of Earth for ever, Rawgug's military training kicked in. First, they had to colonise the Moon by breeding, which meant some loving words for Malwog.

'&*&*$$$^^≥≥≥÷÷√√√∂ƒß†®¨¥¥¥¨ø¥•¶∞¢#€ åß∂´ƒ˙¬^!!!'

Martian sex works quickly, and in no time there were forty-five of them. Step two required a Martian joke.

')(%*¥√¨˙ ÏÊÁ^^ÎÓÔ˜°°√ç¨∆!' said Rawgug, loudly.

Malwog died laughing, literally; colonisation was complete.

DOES FLASH GORDON LIVE HERE?

The doorbell rang: the postman, wearing a full set of chain mail armour.

'Can you help me, sir?' he asked. Seeing my bemused look, he explained, 'It's the new Royal Mail uniform.' Noticing his nameplate, Arthur King, I nodded.

'How can I help?'

'I've got letters for Daniel Dare, Flash Gordon, Batman and Spiderman. Do they live here?'

I chuckled. 'I think it's a joke. No-one with those names lives here.'

Closing the door, I caught myself in the hall mirror. Realising that my blue and red cape was ruffled, I patted down the giant yellow 'S' on my front.

DOES EVERYONE GET THESE?

The old lady allowed herself an evil chuckle.

She'd printed a number of emails sent to her that previous week. Each asked her to log in to her bank accounts with HSBC, Barclays, RBS, JP Morgan Chase and Citibank, then follow a series of instructions 'to resolve some ongoing security issues'. But she had accounts with none of them.

But she did have special skills. She could combine an extraordinary range of keys to allow her to manipulate any computer connected to hers.

Five minutes later, each of the phishing computers had burst into flames and destroyed their owners' homes.

I wish.

IT'S WRITTEN IN THE STARS

Hydra looked lovingly across the night sky towards Orion.

'I love big strong-looking men,' she said.

'I like your hair,' he replied. 'Different styles on each head.'

'I've just had them cut,' she said. 'Do you like them?'

'More than ever.' Then Orion summoned all his courage. 'I love you. Will you marry me?'

'Of course,' she replied in chorus. 'I love you too. Shall we set a date?'

Of course, celestial pillow-talk is very slow; remember they're zillions of light years apart. It was all they'd time for before all their stars were dead.

It's tough being a constellation.

Horror

SWEET DREAMS

Amy awoke to knocking on her bedroom window. She'd slept poorly since Matt had left her; tonight's gale-force winds made things worse.

Assuming that the tapping was merely the wind tapping tree branches against her window, Amy nevertheless rose, defiantly throwing back the curtains.

At first – nothing; then a dark shape emerged from the pitch-black night. She could only see its eyes. Then, with a deep unpleasant laugh, it transformed into Matt.

'Let me in, Amy, please,' said Mark. Entranced, she opened the window.

Next morning Amy's body was found in bed; every organ had been sucked from her body.

FORTHCOMING ATTRACTION

Concentrate on your tablet, laptop or PC screen: one hundred words isn't a lot, each one has to count.

Relax, make yourself comfortable. Let yourself relax in the chair, let it fit your body like a glove.

It feels good, that chair, doesn't it? Can you feel it starting to take hold of you? That chair is alive, it wants you, it's going to swallow you just as it's devoured so many innocents before you. You're dinner. There's no escape.

And whatever you do, don't look behind you. Something else is there, waiting, especially for you.

THE UNRINGING

As Halloween's end approached, the tiny village of St Egbert's collectively shivered. Nobody knew who rang the church bell – everyone was past caring anyway, trusting in prayer instead.

Each year at midnight, the bell struck twelve then continued, fifteen, perhaps sixteen strikes, each extra stroke representing a soul taken. Those hearing the bells ring were safe for another year, otherwise...

This year was a bad one. Neither Mrs Clancy nor Jim Pearce heard bells. Bess Merryweather's cancer finally claimed her, too. But losing the two Dempsey boys, speeding on the back road in their parents' car, that was too much.

THE DOOR

They'd lived there for three years but never once opened the third bedroom's cupboard door. When they'd bought the house, they'd been told that a dark secret lay behind it.

The door was locked – the key long-lost – and painted over many times. Henry was convinced the door was a trompe l'oeil. There simply wasn't space for a cupboard, there was simply nothing there.

Jennifer wasn't so sure. One evening, determined to discover the truth, she instructed Henry to open the door with a crowbar. Fully ten minutes later, it finally gave way.

What they saw made their blood run cold.

TRICK OF THE LIGHT?

It might have been a trick of the light.

Watching television, I gradually started to sense that the figures on the screen weren't the only things moving in the room. I couldn't be sure, but it seemed that the subjects in the photographs on the fireplace and the wall had changed slightly; an altered expression, an adjusted posture, perhaps. My normally-gentle sister Jan appeared angry. Auntie Emma seemed to be frowning instead of smiling. Ann-Louise, my ex-wife, seemed to be holding something in her lap: a revolver? She certainly wasn't smiling, for sure.

Then I realised someone was behind me.

THE DOOR IN THE BASEMENT

He studied the basement cupboard door before him. Locked for years, he'd no idea if it was empty, even what size it was. Probably walk-in, but one could never be sure. They'd bought the house without getting a chance to see inside. But where there's a will...

So here he was, clutching some skeleton keys he'd borrowed from a local locksmith. Something must fit, and sure enough, at the fifth attempt, the lock turned crustily. Gingerly, he opened the door.

He still wasn't prepared for what he found.

Managing to compose himself, he called out, 'Sally, we have a problem.'

FOREST HALT

Jack knew the line well. Running along the hillside, it cut through a heavily-forested area, clearing briefly to give a stunning view of the valley.

One night as the train passed the clearing, Jack thought he spotted a disused station, Forest Halt, on the opposite side from the view. He wasn't sure, though, it just flashed past.

At the depot, Jack asked about Forest Halt, but no-one had ever noticed it.

Next evening, when Jack's train was on the line again, an ill-timed landslide carried all three coaches down the steep embankment. No-one survived. Forest Halt was never seen again.

LUNCH AT THE VAMPIRES' GUILD

The Vampires' Guild was holding its annual vegetarian buffet lunch. One woman had ignored all advice and had more kale than was good for her; now she was hallucinating.

'My queendom for a pasty,' she slurred. 'My queendom for a pasty!'

Someone popped a piece of kale-wasabi cake into the woman's mouth. It had a dramatic effect: she had a seizure and lay writhing on the floor.

'Give her blood, give her blood,' the cry went up. Two Guild committee members flew to the woman to apply neck-to-mouth rescusitation. It did the trick; ten minutes later she was drinking tea.

SNAKE

Thirty thousand feet into the air is no place to discover that a coastal taipan, the world's third most deadly snake, is loose in the passenger cabin. We're mid-Pacific, which makes sense given that we're flying from Sydney to Los Angeles, but anyone unfortunate enough to be bitten won't make it; untreated bites kill within ninety minutes – always – and the Quantas flight is many hours from landing yet.

The pilot has sensibly locked the cockpit door, but in no time the panicked snake slips underneath it and strikes both pilot and co-pilot immediately.

The flight now has a real problem.

Sport And Leisure

EMILY'S DRIVING TEST
WINTER OLYMPICS, 2022
THE KILLING FIELDS
DEMI ON THE CATWALK
THE BEGINNINGS OF GOLF
THE OPEN GOLF CHAMPIONSHIP
PUTTING FOR FOUR
ADDICTION
EXTRA-HOT MINCED BEEF CURRY

EMILY'S DRIVING TEST

Emily winced.

The driving examiner getting into the passenger seat was the dreaded 'Pink Dragon', so-called because she was (a) pink and (b) a dragon. Despite desperate efforts to control her flaming breath with peppermints, she'd already torched seventy-eight cars, each time prematurely ending the candidate's chances of success.

The test proceeded quietly, the dragon calling instructions through the open window. Then, half-way through, she called for Emily to preform the required sudden emergency stop, always a risky moment for dragons. Emily braked hard; the dragon screamed in fright.

That made it seventy-nine. But Emily got her entry fee back.

WINTER OLYMPICS, 2022

Written just after Canada had banned the importation of some famous Scottish products.

Because nobody could afford to host the 2022 Winter Olympics, the newly-independent Scotland had agreed to step in to fill the gap. Running the entire event using Skype, Wie and Dance Mats, none of the competitors even had to leave their native lands.

Sadly, the host nation were as useless as ever, claiming their first gold medals only on the last day. From living-room armchairs in front of their televisions, they won both men's and women's curling gold medals, beating Canada in the final each time.

Next day the Scots were all disqualified, testing positive for a banned substance: Irn-Bru.

THE KILLING FIELDS

They stood to attention, in massed serried ranks. They were perhaps a little green, but there was unity in strength and they were developing fast. Already, it felt as though they had a good hold on their position.

They hadn't counted on the electric monster about to be unleashed on them. They heard it first – a great roar from their left, then their right, then their left again – before they saw it. And by the time they saw it, it was too late.

When the mower had gone, row upon row lay fallen, decapitated.

Perhaps they'd fare better next week.

DEMI ON THE CATWALK

Demi appeared confident as she marched down the Milan catwalk, but she was worried. She'd spotted it on each of her four previous forays to the end of the stage, and back, too. It really shouldn't have been a problem, but now the lighting had been darkened to show off her dazzlingly-sequined dress.

Then it happened. Her stilleto heel went straight into the tiny hole left in the floor by a careless set-constructor. At first she tripped to an abrupt halt, then the ultimate nightmare – the heel sheared off completely, leaving her feeling as naked as the day she was born.

THE BEGINNINGS OF GOLF

The discovery that dinosaurs played golf rocked the world of palaeontology to its very core.

Scientists believe that golf really became popular in the Jurassic era. Clubs were made of bone; balls were mostly fashioned from lava, although meteorite-balls were all the rage amongst the velociraptor jet-set. Courses rarely featured water, but desert was common; almost all championship golf took place near erupting volcanos. Dinosaur golf was dominated by 'The Big Three': Diplodocus, Brachiosaurus, and of course, Tyrannosaurus.

Sadly, a catastrophic event – perhaps an asteroid hitting Earth – wiped out almost all golfing dinosaurs. Only those that found shelter in the old clubhouses survive today.

THE OPEN GOLF CHAMPIONSHIP

There was – by Plutonian standards – great excitement as the Plutonian Golf Open Championship approached. Golf was relatively new to the planet, developed initially for Neptunian holidaymakers.

However, ten years previously sponsors funded an annual Plutonian Open, and this year the whole planet was buzzing with excitement over rumours that the new Earth wunderkind, Jordan Spieth, was going to take part. Success on Pluto would complete the Solar Grand Slam, and crowds lined up in the streets to await his arrival by the spaceship New Horizons.

There was therefore great disappointment when the craft flew on past the planet without landing...

PUTTING FOR FOUR

Nearly eighty, Mike played golf daily. But golf brought torments: he simply couldn't putt, wrecking scores with frequent missed putts.

One morning he announced to everyone, 'I'm terminally ill, boys. Cancer.'

'That's terrible,' his friends cried

'Don't worry,' Mike said, 'I've got years left yet. Apparently I'll die of something else first.'

Just then, he tapped in a short putt. 'That's a – '

'FORE!' The shout from behind was too late – Mike was killed instantly.

The funeral was well-attended. At Mike's request, his ashes were buried in a hole on the 18th green. They missed trying to pour them in.

ADDICTION

He came through the door of the living room carrying the foil-wrapped package she craved so badly. She felt her pulse quicken in anticipation of the coming hit.

He held it in front of her, just out of reach.

'Bastard,' she yelled. 'Give it here!'

'Cash on delivery. That cost me money,' her supplier said slyly. Power. She threw some cash at him, snatched the package, unwrapped it greedily.

Within seconds, the effects coursed through every part of her.

Then: guilt. As always, she swore she would make this her last time. But she knew chocolate was winning the battle.

EXTRA-HOT MINCED BEEF CURRY

This is a recipe I've tried myself.

Dry-fry six ground cloves, a stick of cinnamon and a half-teaspoon of ground cardamom in a saucepan until the mixture smokes.

Then add some sunflower oil to the smoking spices and a finely-chopped onion. Sauté slowly until soft, then add 500g minced beef, stirring until browned. Add 2 teaspoons ground coriander and fenugreek, one teaspoon each of ground cumin, garlic powder and turmeric, a half-teaspoon each of ginger and chilli powder, some tomato puree and a little salt. Add 300ml beef stock.

Leave over a low gas to cook. Forget about it for six hours then call the Fire Brigade.

Christmas

READY FOR SANTA CLAUS

She was convinced that Santa Claus was an illegal immigrant, a terrorist and that his sack contained a bomb with which to blow up everyone up. She also believed he was a muslim, of which his long white beard was proof.

But our hero didn't lack courage, no! On social media she fearlessly posted capitalised rants demanding Santa's repatriation. She'd be READY AND WAITING when he came.

On Christmas Eve, she waited for him in the dark. Just after midnight, a hooded figure slipped down the chimney.

But the hooded figure wasn't carrying a sack, he was carrying a scythe.

CHRISTMAS MARK II

Abandoned long ago by judgemental friends and family, a heavily-pregnant young woman arrived one night in a little village. Those few passers-by who noticed her wandering around assumed she was drunk. No-one offered help, far less accommodation.

She found shelter in a large overturned communal dustbin, and that night somehow gave birth to a baby girl. As the baby suckled, her mother said to her, 'Cheer up, love, this is as good as it gets. Perhaps the next life's better.'

They found out soon enough; a severe night-time freeze carried them both off. But they were together to the end.

BREAKDOWN

Santa was unable to deliver parcels, and this time it wasn't a fairy story, it was for real. For the first time ever, he had to call the emergency rescue services.

'It's Blitzen,' he explained. 'He's gone lame – I think it's his long-standing arthritis. Whatever, the sleigh's pulling to the left badly and we're literally going round in circles. We can't get south of Helsinki.'

Eventually, the rescue service turned up, looking suspiciously like a polar bear. In no time, it had solved the problem by eating both Blitzen AND Donner.

The sleigh was going straight again, Santa was happy.

NATIVITY SCENE No.1

'Sure you got the address right?' asked Bally. He and Caz were getting irritated.

'Stable Lane,' snapped Mel.

'Lotta money riding on this, Mel,' Caz said, threateningly.

'I'm doin' my best. Even Land Rovers have to go easy towing caravans.'

'I ain't losing to hicks on foot.'

'They're not on foot,' Bally said. 'Those guys are professional shepherds – they use quad bikes.'

Caz cursed. 'Well we've got your sat-nav. They'll never find that Travelodge in Bethlehem.'

Suddenly, Bally pointed skywards. 'What's that? Sure is bright.'

Mel gasped. 'That's the International Space Station. They're following that!'

Caz cursed again. 'That's cheating.'

A POSSIBLE EXPLANATION FOR ONE OF THE BIBLE'S GREAT LATE ARRIVALS

Three wise men were waiting patiently for the trans-desert express.

Jimmy said, 'Thankfully we're old enough to get free travel nowadays, boys. The cost of the fares is skyrocketing.'

'What's your gift?' Tam asked. 'I'm taking chocolate coins wrapped in gold paper.'

'Frankinsence deodorant,' Jimmy replied. 'You, Willie?'

'Myrrh baby lotion.'

Suddenly, they were blinded by a dazzling light in the sky. Fumbling vainly for their spectacles, they realised too late that their bus was sailing past their stop - without them.

'Damn,' said Jimmy. 'When's the next one?'

Willie checked the app on his mobile. 'Twelve days from now.

INTERNET DATING AT CHRISTMAS

It all seemed so promising to start with. We'd met through www.findmyperfectpartner.com and we seemed so suited, despite the fact that we lived thousands of miles apart.

Then, around Christmas, gifts started to appear, each arriving on successive days ordered from Amazon. At first it was just a series of birds – well, you can always eat them – apart from five bits of bling that came one day. But suddenly the gifts became bizarre: eight milkmaids, then some men and women seemingly on amphetamines.

Then, one morning, pipes and drums smashed out beneath my bedroom window. Our brief romance was over.

APPLICATION FOR POST WITH AMAZON

WHAT SPECIAL APTITUDES, EXPERIENCE AND QUALIFICATIONS MAKE YOU SUITED TO THIS POSITION?

I have many years' experience in worldwide retail deliveries and distribution, mainly self-employed. I can maintain inventories, and match customer demand request forms accurately, even in quite high volume situations. I am used to working under pressure and am prepared to continue doing so, including undertaking night shift work where necessary. I have considerable experience of managing a transport fleet.

I have a Level 5 qualification in Reindeer Care.

WHAT SPECIAL REQUIREMENTS MIGHT YOU HAVE FROM US?

Pension scheme.

OTHER RELEVANT INFORMATION

Currently laid off until next December.

THE HOUR OF THE ANGELS

Why does nobody understand the power –
literally – of Christmas tree lights?

When strings of lights hang around the tree and
they're left on for any length of time, magnetic
fields build up around the entire circuit. It might
not seem much, but over the hours that little
trickle is enough to bring life to those dormant
angels hanging on the tree alongside them.

The angels on the tree are ready, believe me.
They'll move in the dead of night, sliding silently
from room to room until they find their prey.

Did you switch the lights off? Are you sleeping
comfortably?

Miscellaneous

BAD NEWS AT THE DOCTOR'S

The doctor sat down facing the patient directly; he wore a serious expression and the patient knew something was wrong.

'Let me have it straight, doc. What's the problem?'

The doctor shook his head. 'You seem to have caught diabetes 2. Your blood tests show that your chromosomes have altered irrevocably, I'm afraid.'

'Diabetes 2? But how?'

'It can come from a virus, or an insect bite. Or too much internet shopping.'

The patient sighed. 'The perils of modern life, I suppose.'

'Indeed,' said the doctor.

'Is there any hope?'

'No, your chromosomes indicate that you've already become a zombie.'

BUTTERFLY

Barely a cloud was visible across the wide expanse of blue sky as, in parks and on beaches, sun-lovers of all ages enjoyed the weather: twenty-seven degrees, the warmest of the year. Many had shed more clothing than perhaps was wise – they'd suffer the next day – but this was good time, time not for working but for friends and family instead. Ice cream stalls were prospering.

Around six, the intense heat turned to a violent thunderstorm, rapidly washing away all signs of earlier pleasure.

And that was it for another year: Britain's summer, one fine day, just like Madame Butterfly.

SHARED EMBARRASSMENT

Once again, this really is a true story.

Invited to Sunday lunch with mutual friends, they made small talk: how each knew the hosts, work, neighbourhood stuff, children and grandchildren, the usual things.

But she knew him from somewhere else, possibly a long-ago one-night stand, perhaps just a neighbour. Then she remembered.

Twenty years previously, he'd taken her daughter and some friends camping. Her daughter's tent had accidentally caught fire and he'd pulled the girl out just in time.

Now she was embarrassed that she hadn't recognised the man who'd saved her daughter's life.

He was still embarrassed that a child in his care had been so endangered.

ONE BORN EVERY MINUTE

The old man was fishing when a tourist came by.

'Successful?'

'Aye,' the old man grunted towards some glittering pieces of rock.

'Is that gold?'

''Salmon swallows it. River's fu' o'gold. Mak' twa hunner every day.' With that, he landed a salmon, extracted a gold nugget from its mouth, then threw the fish back.

'Can I try?' the tourist asked.

'I'll want compensation fur ma lost earnins,' the old man said.

Next day, the tourist returned, handed over two hundred pounds and caught nothing. There was no gold or salmon; merely a conjuring trick that earned two hundred pounds daily.

FAILED DELIVERY

The old man lay on the living room carpet, curled in a ball. He said nothing.

Outside at the front door, a delivery man rang the bell. No reply. He tried again, but still the old man didn't answer. The delivery man peered through the letter box, but the house seemed empty. Conscientiously writing out a postcard to say he'd try again later, he posted it; then on his handheld electronic notepad, he recorded the 'failed attempt to deliver'. As he left, he saw no-one in the apartment block hallway.

Someone else would have to discover the old man.

SERVING HER EVERY NEED

The queen bee had called the drones to order. 'Tell me,' she asked, 'exactly *what* is your function around here?'

The drones spoke in unison. 'Our duty is to obey, Your Majesty. Our duty is to serve your every need. Our duty is to otherwise loiter about and let the women do all the work.'

'So… do I really need you? I mean, apart from a little bit of hanky-panky now and then… and I could settle for a vibrator.'

Suddenly, the drones formed themselves into a giant boy-band, singing: 'It Don't Mean A Thing If It Ain't Got Wing…'

THE REAL REASON WHY KINDLES WERE INVENTED

The large book coffee-table book contained representations of the strange four-dimensional photodrawings by the Explorationists. Malkowski's famous 'Ford Futuritica' was there, the car which seemed to go in all directions at the same time, yet further study transformed the car into a horse or spaceship. Jeanne Dubuisson's Eliptical Square was there, so too Mark Leonard's Gateway To Heaven in the shape of a recycling bin.

Peering, Dorothy was drawn ever closer, until her face touched the page. Then, quietly, the book closed its covers around her and she was never seen again. She was the book's ninth victim that month.

THE GREATEST STORY EVER

Dragons, it turns out, have extraordinary powers to move emotions, especially when they choose to write. On the last day in May, Albert The Dragon came up with a tale to make any human cry: tears of laughter, tears of sadness, tears of joy, all within the space of one hundred words. Reading back through it, Albert realised he had created his masterpiece, the greatest piece of fiction ever constructed.

'Ahhh,' he said, reading the printout of his story. Sadly, his breath set fire to the paper, and in the ensuing panic he forgot it completely, and for all time.

THE OLD CRONE

She was a sad case.

Perhaps she'd outlived her time, for her sole remaining joy seemed to lie in criticising others.

Sometimes, she wrote letters to her neighbours detailing their faults: anonymously, naturally, but everyone in the community knew who'd sent them. If chided, she claimed she was 'only joking', but no-one was fooled. Once, she'd have been a candidate for the ducking-stool; these days townsfolk just spoke about her behind her back.

She died alone, her body lying undiscovered for several days before anyone noticed.

Pity, really: she wasn't all bad, she just went off-colour towards her life's end.

A STUDY IN YELLOW

More true stuff. Do you mind?

We found him face down wearing a yellow outdoor coat and a pair of bright yellow wellington boots.

'Is he OK, do you think?' Ruth asked me. 'I can't hear him breathing.'

I listened too, could hear nothing. I decided to be honest. 'How should I know?'

'Should we waken him to check?' she suggested. I snorted a response: 'Rather you than me.'

Ten minutes later, Ruth did waken him, even tried lifting him from his cot. By now he was screaming, refusing to allow the coat and boots to come off. Yellow was staying.

Two-year-olds know their mind.

GUESS WHAT HAPPENED AT WORK TODAY?

So this woman comes into my office to claim benefits for the first time. Claims she's a redundant 'hitperson'! Honestly!

Turns out I've a job for her – involving a cat somehow – but she throws a tantrum. 'I have standards,' she announces. So I say, no benefits for you, sweetheart. Off she strops.

In no time she's back. 'I claim religious discrimination,' she announces. She's a Quaker, a pacifist hitperson. Seriously. No can kill.

I mention Grace Kelly in *High Noon* but she replies Grace only killed baddies. Then she draws a gun out saying, 'Like you.'

She gets her benefits.

THE PLUTONIAN GENERAL ELECTION

In Plutonian elections, everyone is a candidate but only seven wise people vote, so winners are chosen sensibly from the best candidates.

This year's Election Debate was a lengthy affair. Each candidate was asked, 'What is the meaning of life?' Being politicians, they avoided answering the question. The Brown Party warned that Pluto's changing climate meant it would end up green and blue. The Plutonian Planetary Party wanted Pluto's planetary status restored. A nasty man blamed everything on Uranian and Neptunian immigrants. But most just wanted better services or lower taxes.

The ruling government was returned with an increased majority.

\

'WASTE OF TIME FRIDAY'

Today, if you didn't know, is 'Waste of Time Friday'.

It's the day when your Inbox is entirely full of pointless emails, and when your boss summons you to a meeting, it has nothing to do with you. It's the day when you go clothes-shopping and find nothing that suits. It's the day when you go to the cash machine but it's broken. Today, the evening meal you're cooking burns, and has to be thrown out.

Any minute now you'll discover this story has more than 100 words. Go on, check it.

Told you it was 'Waste of Time Friday'.

NEARLY THE END

Acknowledgements

Thanks for reading, assuming you've got this far. If you enjoyed it, it would really help if you could drop a quick review at one or more of the many sites such as Amazon, Smashwords, Goodreads – the list is endless. Come to think of it, even if you didn't like it, feel free to say so online. Authors develop thick skins.

A fair few folk have helped bring this collection into existence, most of them unwittingly it has to be said. Chief amongst these has to be Emma Baird. Author of the excellent young adult novel *Katie And The Deelans,* plus two other novels on the brink of publication at time of writing, she's also the founder of Friday Flash Fiction; it's from her head that this entire 100-word story nonsense emerged. As the Creative Director of Comely Bank Publishing she's also acted in an editorial capacity, checking that this collection is up to the organisation's quality standards. Blame her if you thought the stories were rubbish, then.

However it would be wrong not to acknowledge the comments of many other contributors to Friday Flash Fiction. There are really too many to mention, but some of the longer-lasting ones have included Russell Conover, Joy Essien, Amy Friedman, Jan Jorgensen, Len Nourse, Jo Oldani-Osborne, Jane Reid, Eric Smith and Bobby Warner. I'd particularly recommend Eric Smith's recently-published memoir, written in vignette style, called *Not A Bad Ride.* But if you take a look at the Friday Flash Fiction website you'll see that each writer has or her own style and you can see for yourself which you prefer. You can even have a go yourself.

As ever, my wife Katherine has had to sit across the living room from me while I've sat with my laptop selecting wheat from chaff and assembled them into an ebook. She seems content enough reading newspapers, doing crosswords, and listening to all sorts of music on her iPad, but her company's been great throughout.

About The Author

Born in 1952, Gordon Lawrie has lived his entire life in Edinburgh working as a secondary school teacher until he quit in 2011 to dabble in writing fiction. Fiction proved to be a relief from writing supposedly serious articles on citizenship or reviewing other writers' work on education, and his first novel *Four Old Geezers And A Valkyrie* was published, first as an ebook in 2012, then in print the following year.

Other work followed, including short stories, some poetry and numerous flash fiction works of varying length, but specialising mainly in 'drabbles', stories of exactly 100 words in length.

Today, in addition to his writing, he works as a part-time IT and website consultant, manages the website for Friday Flash Fiction, and is Founder and Managing Director of the self-publishing collective Comely Bank Publishing.

Also By The Author

FOUR OLD GEEZERS AND A VALKYRIE

Gordon Lawrie's first published novel is an entertaining romp set in contemporary Edinburgh.

Brian, aka 'Captain', is a recently-retired, disillusioned teacher who has split acrimoniously with his ex-wife, known for a wild temper and throwing things at him. In his rush to get free of her, he has mistakenly agreed to give her half of his newly-acquired pension, seriously threatening his precarious finances. A chance meeting with his best man encourages Captain to dig out his forty-year-old guitar and leads to some hilarious jam sessions during which they record a couple of Captain's own songs.

Posting these on YouTube, they prove to be surprise hits, sending the four 'musicians' and their lawyer into a series of encounters with a tiny manager, a boy-band and a female Polish dancer, a cigar-puffing earl and a famous rock band.

The novel is unusual in that the songs Captain writes really exist, and most of them can be downloaded, either in sheet-music form or as downloadable mp3 files, at the author's website.

Available at all good bookshops or online, including at
www.lawrie.info

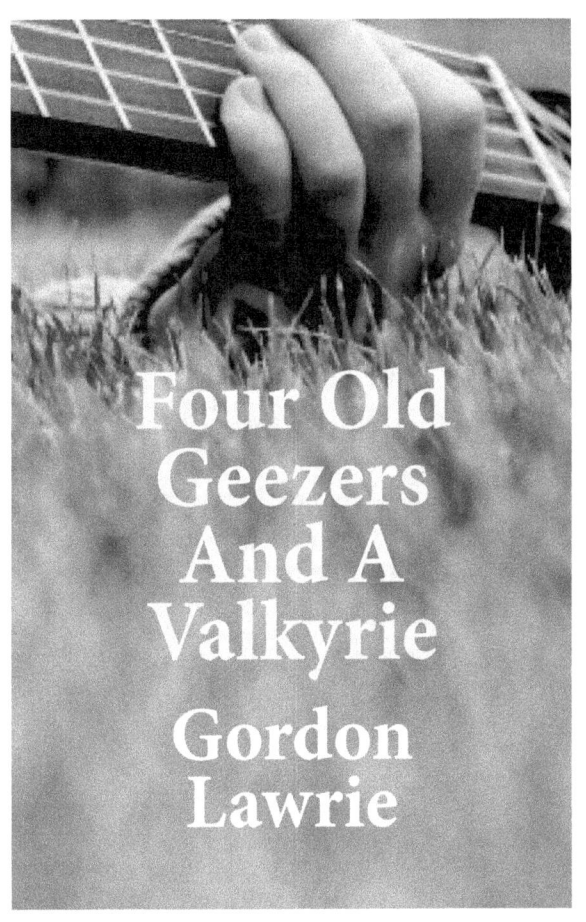

Four Old Geezers And A Valkyrie

Gordon Lawrie

THE DISCREET CHARM OF MARY MAXWELL-HUME

The Discreet Charm of Mary Maxwell-Hume, published in 2017 is Gordon Lawrie's first novella.

Mary Maxwell-Hume is an enigma. She earns a living as a piano teacher, but also belongs to an obscure order of nuns. Their rules appear curious: although the nuns wear red habits occasionally, the order has peculiar dress rules: they wear "only as much as is necessary to preserve due modesty", plus liberal doses of Chanel No.5 perfume. There's the faintest hint that Mary might be a con woman, but she uses her sensual powers in such a way that nobody really minds except for the odious Theodore Plews of Lamberts Auction House in Edinburgh. Anyway, who would dare suggest that a woman of God might not all be all she seems?

Eventually, she engages a young police constable as her faithful "assistant"...

The Discreet Charm of Mary Maxwell-Hume includes, as bonus story, *The Piano Exam*. The book is available worldwide on Amazon.

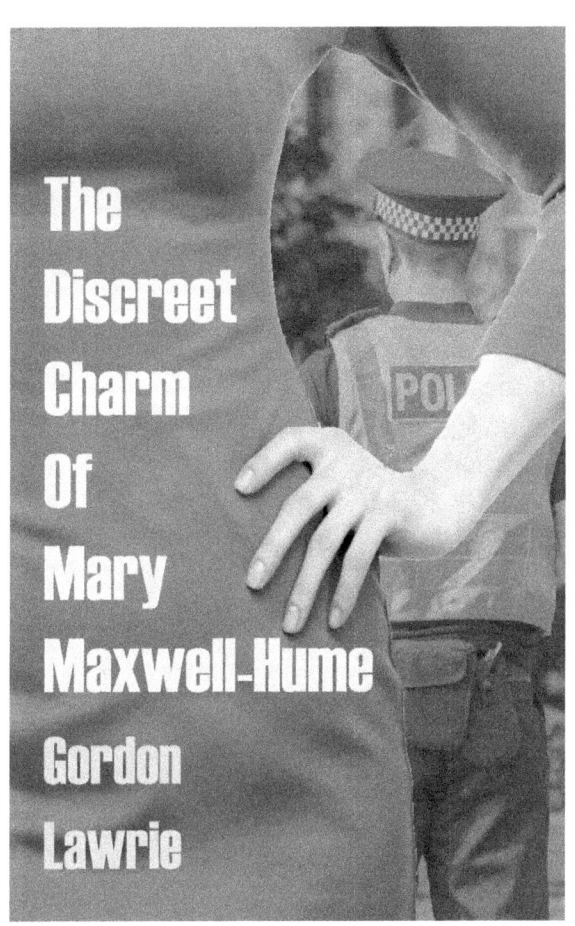

'WHAT'S THE POINT?

One final story: sometimes 100 words is far, far too many.

'Aaaaaarrrrrrrgh!'

'Urrrrrrrrgh!'

'Aaaaaaarrrgh!'

'Uuuuurrrghhh!'

'Aaaaaarrrrgh!'

'Urrrgh!'

'Aaaaarrrrrrgh!'

'Uuuuuuuurrrrgh!'

'AAAAAAAARRRRRGH!'

'Fifteen-love.'